Dear Peter Rabbit

Books by Alma Flor Ada

The Gold Coin
Serafina's Birthday
My Name Is María Isabel
The Unicorn of the West
Dear Peter Rabbit

Books by Leslie Tryon

Albert's Alphabet
Albert's Play
One Gaping Wide-Mouthed Hopping Frog
Albert's Field Trip

Dear Peter Rabbit

by **Alma Flor Ada**

illustrated by **Leslie Tryon**

ATHENEUM 1994 NEW YORK

Maxwell Macmillan Canada
Toronto
Maxwell Macmillan International
New York Oxford Singapore Sydney

Text copyright © 1994 by Alma Flor Ada
Illustrations copyright © 1994 by Leslie Tryon

Atheneum
Macmillan Publishing Company
866 Third Avenue
New York, NY 10022

Maxwell Macmillan Canada, Inc.
1200 Eglinton Avenue East
Suite 200
Don Mills, Ontario M3C 3N1

Macmillan Publishing Company is part of the
Maxwell Communication Group of Companies.

First edition
Printed in the United States of America
10 9 8 7 6 5 4 3 2 1
The illustrations are rendered in pen and ink with watercolor.
Book design by Kimberly M. Adlerman

Library of Congress Cataloging-in-Publication Data
Ada, Alma Flor.
Dear Peter Rabbit / by Alma Flor Ada; illustrated by Leslie
Tryon.—1st ed.
p.   cm.
Summary: Presents letters between such fairy tale characters as
Goldilocks, Baby Bear, Peter Rabbit, and the Three Pigs.
ISBN 0-689-31850-2
[1. Characters and characteristics in literature—Fiction.
2. Letters—Fiction.] I. Tryon, Leslie, ill. II. Title.
PZ7.A1857De   1994
[E]—dc20   93-8459

Printed on recycled paper

To Timothy Paul
IN HIS SECOND MONTH OF LIFE
—A. F. A.

Dearest Darling Hilda
—L. T.

Straw House
Woodsy Woods
March 12

Peter Rabbit
Rabbit's Burrow
Hollow Oak

Dear Peter,

Have I got news for you! You know how much I've always wanted to have my own house. Well, last week I got lucky. I met a farmer with a big load of hay who offered to let me have some. Pig Two is still working on his stick house, and Pig Three is taking forever to finish his brick house. But my beautiful straw house is all finished and ready!

I will be having a housewarming party next Thursday the nineteenth at 5:00 P.M. So please hop on over and help warm up my house. See you there!

Your good friend,

Pig One

Bear House in the Woods
Hidden Meadows
March 16

Goldilocks McGregor
McGregor's Farm
Vegetable Lane

Dear Goldilocks,

Your letter is *the best*! My grandma always sends a Christmas card and a birthday card, but yours is the first real letter I've ever gotten. *Wow!*

I am sorry that you broke my chair too. It is my most favorite chair. But don't worry. My father fixed it and painted it green because green is my favorite color. Dad says the chair is so strong now that it won't break even if you sit on it again.

Mom says come visit anytime. Dad says it's okay too, but knock on the door first before you come in.

Let me know when you are coming. I'll ask Mom to make us some chocolate cake. She makes the *best* chocolate cake in the whole world!

Your new friend,

Baby Bear

McGregor's Farm
Vegetable Lane
March 19

Baby Bear
Bear House in the Woods
Hidden Meadows

Dear Baby Bear,

   My parents gave me permission to go to your house on Sunday the twenty-second. But I have to remember to water my ten rows of vegetables first.

   It's not that easy to water the garden. The rows are really long, and the watering can is pretty heavy when it's full. But it's kind of fun toward the end of each row. Sometimes when the sun is shining, it makes a little rainbow right there, as I'm making it rain over the vegetables.

   Lately some vegetables have been disappearing from our garden. Every other night or so, a cabbage, a lettuce, or a carrot is missing. My father thinks it's the rabbits that steal them, and it makes him very angry.

   And guess what? Yesterday, after he chased a rabbit out of the garden, my father found a tiny jacket by the fence, and the tiniest pair of shoes between some rows of carrots. He made a little scarecrow with them, and he says he hopes that it will keep the pest away. (I would really like to meet their owner someday.)

   See you Sunday!

Love,

Goldilocks

Rabbit's Burrow
Hollow Oak
March 19

Pig One
Straw House
Woodsy Woods

Dear Pig One,

I am very sorry that I can't be at your housewarming party. I've never been to a housewarming party before, and I'd love to go. But I'm in bed with a cold, and Mother says that as long as I'm sneezing and coughing I can't go anywhere at all.

I was happy to hear your good news, but I myself haven't been very lucky lately. On my last visit to the McGregors' vegetable farm, I almost got caught by Mr. McGregor. I had to jump into a watering can half-full of water in order to hide, and I guess that's how I got this awful cold. Now instead of having fun at your party, I'm in bed drinking chamomile tea.

Your friend,

Peter Rabbit

Stick House
Woodsy Woods
March 20

Peter Rabbit
Rabbit's Burrow
Hollow Oak

Dear Peter,

I'm sorry that you have a cold. But don't feel bad about missing the housewarming party. There wasn't one! Instead I had the most terrible scare. Even now, all of the hairs of my chinny-chin-chin curl up with fear when I think about what happened!

Can you imagine who came knocking at the door? The Big Bad Wolf. Since I refused to open the door and let him in, he started huffing and puffing, and would you believe, he blew my whole house down! There was straw flying everywhere. Fortunately, I managed to escape in one piece to my brother Pig Two's house. I'm living here for now, and since his house is made out of sticks, we should be safe.

The good news is that we will be having a housewarming party for this house next Wednesday, the twenty-fifth. If you are feeling better, please come!

Your friend,

Pig One

Baby Bear
Bear House in the Woods
Hidden Meadows

Dear Baby Bear,

You were so right! Your mother's chocolate cake was delicious. It was a lot of fun to see you. And your father sure knows how to tell stories. I especially like it when he pretends to be a wolf.

Speaking of wolves, I saw the strangest thing when I was coming home from your house. There was a little girl in the forest, all dressed in red, and she was talking to a wolf! He seemed like he was a very nice wolf, not a mean or a scary one. I wanted to talk with him too, but he left before I had a chance.

The little girl told me she was picking flowers to take to her grandmother. I helped her for a little while but then I had to go home. I didn't want to be late, because I didn't want my parents to get mad and tell me I can't come visit you again.

I need to go water the cauliflowers now. I hope you can come visit me sometime!

Love,

Goldilocks

Rabbit's Burrow
Hollow Oak
March 25

Pig One and Pig Two
Stick House
Woodsy Woods

Dear Pig One and Pig Two,

What bad luck! Here I am missing another housewarming party. Are you having ice cream? I sure wish I could be there. But my mother says, "Absolutely not!" I can't get out of bed as long as I'm coughing. And no matter how hard I try not to, it seems I always cough when she's nearby. (Just between you and me, I think that she's afraid I might go back to the McGregors' garden, even though I promised her I wouldn't.) I do hope both of you are having lots of fun. As soon as I am better, I'll come visit your new house.

Love,

Peter Rabbit

P.S. Sorry about the straw house!

Brick House
Woodsy Woods
March 27

Peter Rabbit
Rabbit's Burrow
Hollow Oak

Dear Peter,

You'll never believe what happened! There we were, getting ready for the party, and who shows up again but the very same Big Bad Wolf .

Of course my brother refused to open the door. We thought that in a stick house we'd be safe for sure. Although it took him twice as long as last time, after enough huffs and puffs the Big Bad Wolf blew my brother's stick house right down.

Lucky for us, we outran that old wolf and made it safely over to Pig Three's house. Pig Three says he dares that wolf to try to blow his new brick house down.

And since he's sorry that we lost our houses, Pig Three offered to have a special housewarming party for all of us in his house this Sunday.

I hope that you will be able to come this time. There will be three different kinds of ice cream. I'm sending you some of my grandma's eucalyptus cough drops. They always help me.

Your friend,

Pig One

McGregor's Farm
Vegetable Lane
March 30

Baby Bear
Bear House in the Woods
Hidden Meadows

Dear Baby Bear,

Guess what? I'm having a birthday party next Sunday. I know that your mother doesn't usually let you leave the woods, but I hope that just this once she will let you come. It will be extra special to have you there.

Remember I told you about the little girl in red I saw talking to a wolf? Well, we are friends now. You won't believe what happened to her. That wolf was planning to have her for lunch! If it hadn't been for Hans, the woodcutter, things would have ended pretty badly for her. As it was, things ended badly for the wolf.

Please tell Mama Bear that I will take very good care of you, and it will make me very happy to have you at the party.

Your good friend,

Goldilocks

P.S. I hope the little rabbit who has been stealing lettuce from our garden will also be here Sunday. I secretly washed and ironed his jacket and left it by the gate last night, along with an invitation to the party.

Pig One, Pig Two, and Pig Three
Brick House
Woodsy Woods

Dear Pig One, Pig Two, and Pig Three,

I have received the most surprising letter. I'll bet that you could never in a million years guess who it's from. So I'll just have to tell you: It's from a *human being*!

You know that my mother has forbidden us to go to the McGregors' garden. It's a dangerous place.

But the carrots and cabbages are very hard to resist, and yesterday I didn't even have to go inside the garden. I found my jacket and shoes outside the gate, along with a note and two juicy carrots. The note turned out to be an invitation to Goldilocks McGregor's birthday party! Do you think her father knows about this?

Well, I sure would love to see what a human party is like. And the invitation says to bring as many friends as I want. Would the three of you like to come with me this Sunday at 2:00 P.M.?

Your friend,

Peter Rabbit

P.S. The wolf's tail soup you served at the housewarming party was delicious! I was very happy to make it to your party at last.

Wolf Lane
Oakshire
April 4

Mr. Fer O'Cious
Hidden Lane
Wooden Heights
Dark Forest

Dear Cousin Fer,

It was very disturbing to hear of your misadventures, and I join you in grieving for your tail.

My own terrible experience after my encounter with that little girl in red has led me to think that perhaps we would do well to change our diet. It is not a pleasant prospect, but it may be in our own best interest to avoid both young girls and pigs from now on.

I have better tidings regarding your tail. As you can see in the enclosed clipping, you should not have any difficulty in procuring a satisfactory replacement. I understand that it will not be quite the same, but it will allow you to leave the house, engage in company, and be seen in public.

I trust that you will be satisfied with the services of Mr. Raccoon, who has been a dear friend for many years. I look forward to enjoying the pleasure of your company once again, in the very near future.

Affectionately,

Wolfy

Cardinal Cottage
Riding Lane
April 6

Ms. Rose Redding
Cottage in the Woods

Dear Grandma,

I went to a wonderful party Sunday. It was really fun. Goldilocks has very interesting friends.

First there was Baby Bear. I never really believed Goldilocks had been to a bear's house. But there we were, and this little bear appeared at the garden gate. Behind him was this large mother bear. And behind her was the largest bear you can ever imagine. That was Papa Bear.

They left Baby Bear at the gate and went home, but Baby Bear stayed for the whole party. Just as I was getting used to him, another surprising group arrived. Three of them were pigs, who looked almost exactly alike. With them was the cutest little rabbit. He was very well dressed, though his jacket was torn and someone had sewn it back together.

I don't think Mr. McGregor really likes Goldilocks's friends. He looked like he was mad all afternoon, and kept saying that he saw wolves in the woods. That scared me and the pigs a little. They say they never want to see another wolf again for as long as they live.

Mrs. McGregor offered us ice cream and cookies even after we'd eaten the whole cake. Bears and pigs have quite an appetite, but Peter, the little rabbit, ate just as much as they did!

I saved you some heart-shaped cookies. I'll bring them over next time, and don't worry, I won't stray from the trail again.

Much, much love from your granddaughter,

Little Red Riding Hood